ONE TINY TWIG

Story
Dan Rhema

Illustration
Michael Leonard

Mesquite Tree Press

For information about permission
to reproduce selections from this book,
write to:
Permissions, Mesquite Tree Press
P.O. Box 17513
Louisville, KY 40217

Printed in Canada

First printing, August 2003

ISBN 0-9729835-0-3

Book design: Michael Leonard

To Ann Yeargin,
editor, mentor, friend.
D. R.

To Camilla Christabel,
our tiny twig.
M. L.

Emily Twig's fourteenth birthday was about to make history -
family history, that is.

"Emily," said her father, "I have one more present for you."

He handed her a well worn wooden box. "This very special gift has been passed down through many generations of Twigs."

Emily opened the box and a squeal escaped her lips. Nestled within were four silver badges and four photographs. She ran her fingers over the silver stars.

"Are they . . . are they real?" she asked.

"They sure are," her grandfather said. "Way back in the 1800s, when Wyoming was still an untamed frontier, your great-great-great grandfather became our town's first sheriff."

Emily gazed back at the photographs. "The very first sheriff!" she said proudly. "Wait a minute . . . Grandpa, is that you?"

"That's me all right. That picture was taken on the day I earned my detective's badge. Here's my father, Edward Twig, and his father, Virgil Twig. And here is Thomas Twig, the man who started it all, the first sheriff of Hickory Springs, Wyoming."

"But, Grandpa, he sure doesn't look like a sheriff. He's not even wearing a cowboy hat."

"Well, I seem to recall an old family story saying that our Thomas here was the first of our Twigs to come to America."

"Where do you think he came from?" she asked.

"Now that's always been a mystery."

"A mystery . . ." said Emily.　　　　　"The mystery of Thomas Twig."

"Emily, we have some time before we leave for vacation to New York," her mother said. "Why don't you and Grandpa see if you can solve this puzzle from the past?"

Emily peered eagerly at her grandfather. He stared back for a moment, pondering this idea, then a big smile crept across his face. He reached into the box, removed Thomas Twig's badge and pinned it on Emily. "I hereby deputize you as the first Twig Time Traveling Detective!"

A very excited Emily did a very undetective-like dance around the table.

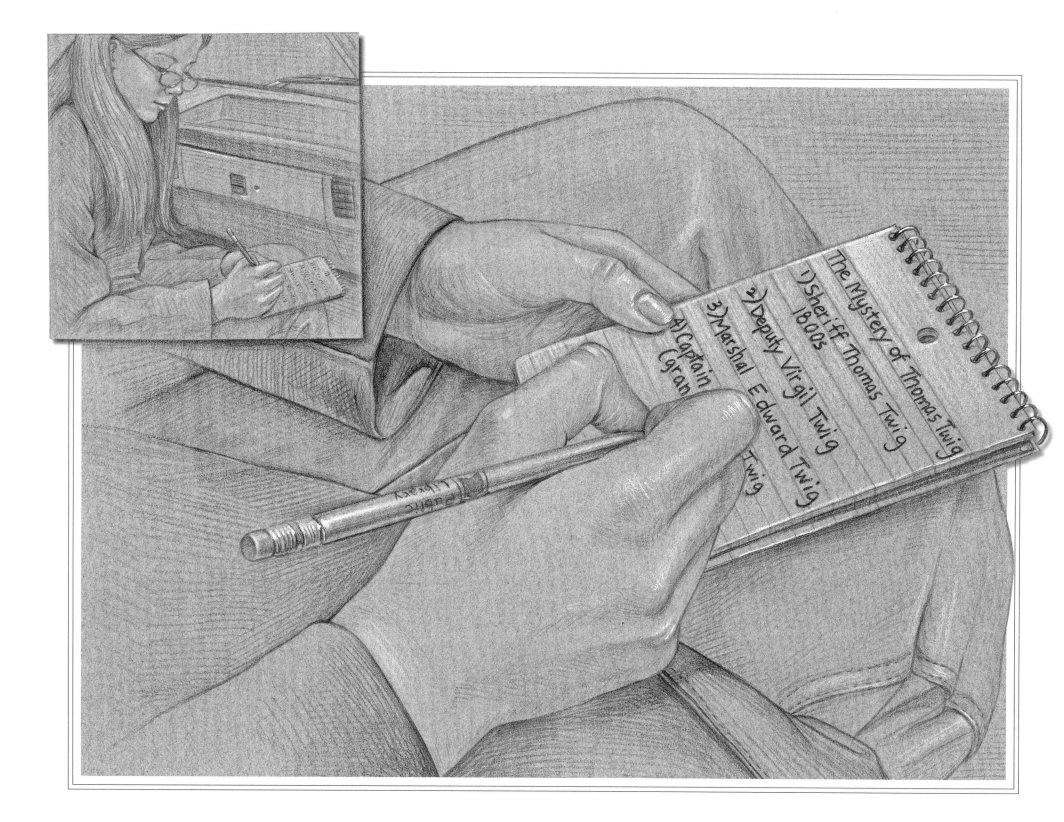

Grandfather Twig arrived bright and early the next morning with one final gift for Emily - an official detective's notebook.

"The key to a proper investigation is keeping track of the facts."

"Thanks, Grandpa. So, where do we begin?" asked Emily as she climbed up into her grandfather's truck.

"Back on the force we used to say, 'Begin with what you know and follow the clues wherever they may lead.'"

Emily flipped open the notebook.

"What *do* we know . . ." she said to herself.

She wrote at the top of the page: The Mystery of Thomas Twig.

Then she began to list the clues.

1. Sheriff Thomas Twig, 1800s
2. Deputy Virgil Twig
3. Marshal Edward Twig
4. Captain James Twig (grandpa)

"Okay, what's next, Grandpa?"

"I've found that when you are searching for someone it helps to put yourself in their place. Try to imagine what Hickory Springs was like during Thomas Twig's time."

Emily gazed through the windshield at the town. In her mind the years began to flash back to the days of the Old West. Cowboys on horseback driving cattle down Main Street appeared before her eyes. And there was Sheriff Thomas Twig, watching over his town.

"Thomas Twig," Emily said out loud, "where did you come from?"

"I don't know the answer to that, Emily," Grandfather replied, "but I do know where he is now." Emily was confused. "I think," he said mysteriously, "that we may discover that our next clue is written in stone."

"Written in stone . . . written in stone . . . wait, I got it. The cemetery! Thomas Twig is in the cemetery."

"Very good, Detective Twig."

"According to our records," said Mrs. Jennings, the cemetery manager, "we have a Thomas and Anna Twig buried right here."

Mrs. Jennings drew a red X on the map.

"Anna Twig!" Emily announced. "Another new clue. She must be my great-great-great grandmother."

Mrs. Jennings handed the map to Emily, then gathered up several large sheets of paper and a large black crayon.

"Let's go see if we can find your Mr. Twig."

Emily used the map to guide the search party through the cemetery.

"This one should be Thomas's and this must be Anna's," said Emily, "but I'm not sure. It's kind of hard to read."

"Here, this may help," said Mrs. Jennings. She placed a sheet of paper over the headstone. "Emily, take the crayon and rub it very gently across the paper."

With every stroke of the crayon, lettering appeared as if by magic.

"Look, it says Thomas . . . Twig." She rubbed a bit more. "Born March 10, 1868! Wow, that was a long time ago!"

"Yes indeed," said her grandfather.

"Should we do Anna's too?" asked Emily.

"Well, if we are going to solve this mystery . . . "

"I know, I know," Emily laughed, "we should follow the clues wherever they may lead."

The very next day the two Twig detectives visited the Hickory Springs courthouse.

"Every ten years since 1790 there has been a counting of the people of the United States," Mr. Osborne, the clerk of the archive, said, as they walked past row upon row of the records of their town and its people.

"Emily, based on the information that you and your grandfather have collected, we should try looking in the 1900 census for your ancestor."

Mr. Osborne disappeared back into the archive returning shortly with a large record book. "Emily, I'm sorry," said Mr. Osborne, "but there wasn't a Thomas Twig listed in the 1900 census for our town." Emily frowned. "But I did find a Thomas Twigg. That's Twig with two gg's."

Emily brightened. "Do you think it could be our Thomas?"

"I wouldn't be surprised," said Mr. Osborne. "It wasn't at all unusual for a family to change the spelling of its name."

TWELFTH CENSUS OF THE UNITED STATES.

SCHEDULE No. 1.—POPULATION.

B

State **Wyoming**

County **Laramie**

Township or other division of county **Hickory Springs Precinct**

Name of incorporated city, town, or village, within the above-named division _____

Supervisor's District No. **300**

Enumeration District No. **42**

Sheet No. **8**

Name of Institution, _____

Ward of city, **X**

Enumerated by me on the **16th** day of June, 1900, **Coy Granville Hampton**, Enumerator.

Line	Dwelling No.	Family No.	NAME	RELATION	Color/race	Sex	Month	Year	Age	Marital	Yrs married	Mother of children	Children living	Birthplace	Father birthplace	Mother birthplace	Yr immigration	Yrs in US	Naturalization	OCCUPATION	Months not employed	Attended school	Can read	Can write	Can speak English	Own/rent	Owned free/mortgaged	Farm/home
51	386	394	Twigg, Thomas J	Head	W M	Mar 1868		32	M 8				England	England	England	1892	8	Na	County Sheriff	0		yes	yes	yes	O	M	H
52			— Anna	Wife	W F	Aug 1870		29	M 8	5	5	Wyoming	Virginia	Maryland							yes	yes	yes			
53			— Virgil E.	Son	W M	Feb 1893		7	S			Wyoming	England	Wyoming				At School	9	yes	yes	yes			
54			— Thomas B.	Son	W M	Jan 1895		5	S			Wyoming	England	Wyoming						no	yes	yes			
55			— Sarah M.	Daughter	W F	Dec 1896		3	S			Wyoming	England	Wyoming											
56			— Anna E.	Daughter	W F	Dec 1896		3	S			Wyoming	England	Wyoming											
57			— Edward L.	Son	W M	May 1898		2	S			Wyoming	England	Wyoming											
58	387	395	Blevins, Edward	Head	W M	Jan 1848		52	M 31			Virginia	Scotland	Germany				Dry Goods Merchant	0		yes	yes	yes	O	F	H
59			— Sarah	Wife	W F	Apr 1853		47	M 31	9	7	Maryland	Maryland	Maryland											
60			— Mary E.	Daughter	W F	June 1884		16	S			Wyoming	Virginia	Maryland				At School	9	yes	yes	yes			
61			— Daniel L.	Son	W M	Oct 1888		11	S			Wyoming	Virginia	Maryland				At School	9	yes	yes	yes			
62			— William M.	Son	W M	Feb 1892		8	S			Wyoming	Virginia	Maryland				At School	9	yes	yes	yes			
63	388	396	Boyd, William	Head	W M	Apr 1853		47	M 11			Canada (Eng.)	Canada	Canada	1877	23	Na	Carpenter	8		no	no	no	O	F	H
64			— Mary B.	Wife	W F	Nov 1863		36	M 11	4	4	California	Kentucky	Missouri							yes	yes	yes			
65			— Michael E.	Son	W M	Mar 1890		10	S			California	Canada	California				At School	9	yes	yes	yes			
66			— Jesse J.	Son	W M	Jan 1892		8	S			California	Canada	California				At School	3½	yes	yes	yes			
67			— Mark B	Son	W M	Sep 1895		4	S			California	Canada	California											
68			— Archibald B	Son	W M	Aug 1897		2	S			Wyoming	Canada	California											
69	389	397	Pierson, James	Head	W M	Nov 1855		44	M 19			Illinois	Norway	Norway				Farmer	0		yes	yes	yes	O	M	F
70			— Maria	Wife	W F	Dec 1863		36	M 19	11	8	Norway	Norway	Norway	1875	25										
71			— Amelia	Daughter	W F	Feb 1886		14	S			North Dakota	Illinois	Norway				At School	9	yes	yes	yes			
72			— Samuel	Son	W M	Mar 1887		13	S			North Dakota	Illinois	Norway				At School	9	yes	yes	yes			
73			— Sandra	Daughter	W F	Apr 1889		11	S			Wyoming	Illinois	Norway				At School	5	yes	yes	yes			
74			— David	Son	W M	Nov 1893		6	S			Wyoming	Illinois	Norway											
75			— Clyde	Son	W M	June 1895		4	S			Wyoming	Illinois	Norway											
76			— Oscar	Son	W M	Mar 1897		3	S			Wyoming	Illinois	Norway											
77			— Harry	Son	W M	July 1898		1	S			Wyoming	Illinois	Norway											
78	390	398	Manuel, Rogers	Head	W M	1842		58	M 28			Portugal	Portugal	Portugal	1865	35	Na	Farmer	0		yes	yes	yes	O	F	F	10
79			— James	Son	W M	Aug 1884		15	S			Wyoming	Portugal	Portugal				Farm Hand	0		yes	yes	yes			

Emily and her grandfather looked at the copy of the census and there he was . . . Thomas Twigg.

"Grandpa, it says that he was thirty-two years old." Emily flipped through her notebook to the dates on the tombstone. "Our Thomas Twig was born in 1868 . . . 1868 plus thirty-two equals 1900! It matches exactly!"

"And here, just under his name," said Grandfather, "is Anna, his wife, and a son named Virgil. It must be Thomas."

"Oh, Grandpa, look, Thomas Twigg was born in England! Our Thomas Twigg was English!"

"Emily Twig, do you realize that you have just solved the mystery of Thomas Twigg, the first sheriff of Hickory Springs?"

"Aww, Grandpa, I couldn't have done it without you," she laughed.

Emily ran her fingers across the census page. She felt as if she was reaching back through time. "Grandpa," she said, "do we have to stop now? Can we keep working on the case after I get back from vacation?"

"Of course we can. I have to admit, this is the most fun I've had in a while."

Emily stared out the airplane window at the land sweeping by beneath the plane. "You're awfully quiet for a girl going on vacation," her father said.
"Oh, I was just wondering about how Thomas Twigg made his way to Hickory Springs."
"He would have come to America by ship - then, I guess, he would have traveled west by train as far as he could and then by horse or stagecoach the rest of the way."
"By ship," her mother said excitedly. "Emily, he came by ship. It's possible that Thomas Twigg passed through Ellis Island on his way to Hickory Springs."
"Ellis Island?" asked Emily.
"Yes, in New York harbor near the Statue of Liberty. It was the place where many immigrants landed in America."
Emily was thrilled. Her family's vacation to New York could end up being the perfect way to continue her investigation into the case of Thomas Twigg.

On Ellis Island, Emily remembered her grandfather's words and tried to imagine Thomas Twigg stepping off a ship into his new country. Later, after a tour of the immigration museum, a staff person showed Emily how to search their computer database.

She entered his name and . . . "Mom . . . Dad," Emily called out. "I found him!" Before her, on the computer screen, was an image of the actual passenger list of the ship *Estelle*. And near the top of the page was Thomas Twigg, a young man of twenty-four years who left his home in Derby, England, traveling to America in 1892.

"Wait till Grandpa hears about this," Emily giggled.

Back home Emily found that her grandfather had been busy too. He asked Emily to meet him at the public library. "Emily, I have a surprise for you," he said. "It's a family history site I found on the Internet. I believe it's time for us to make our family tree."

Emily entered their clues into the computer and the Twig family tree began to grow and grow and grow, reaching back across the Atlantic Ocean to the small English village of Derby.

"Wow!" said Emily.

"My, oh my," said Grandfather, "that sure is a heap of new cousins we've stumbled onto!"

"Grandpa," Emily smiled sweetly, "I think I will invite them all to my next birthday party."

"I don't know about that," he laughed, "but I do believe this calls for a celebration."

Virgil Twigg
born: November 22, 1850
Derby, England
died: December 27, 1908

Elizabeth Brown
born: June 11, 1852
Derby, England
died: January 13, 1912

Edward Blevins
born: January 1848
Virginia
died: March 29, 1916

Sarah Unknown
born: April 17, 1853
Maryland
died: July 25, 1902

Sheriff Thomas Twigg
born: March 10, 1868
Derby, England
died: April 12, 1935

Deputy Virgil Twig
born: February, 1893
Hickory Springs, Wyoming
died: April 5, 1973

Anna Blevins
born: August, 1870
Laramie, Wyoming
died: July 22, 1936

Jane Griggs
born: October 14, 1895
Cheyenne, Wyoming
died: May 31, 1970

Marshal Edward Twig
born: May 9, 1912
Hickory Springs, Wyoming
died: December 14, 1986

Irena Edwards
born: October 14, 1914
St. Louis, Missouri
died: April 28, 2000

Captain James Twig
born: May 9, 1933
Hickory Springs, Wyoming

Sarah Virginia Vane
born: July 10, 1933
Fort Collins, Colorado

Edward Twig
born: June 11, 1954
Hickory Springs, Wyoming

Susan Stockton
born: November 25, 1959
Hickory Springs, Wyoming

Emily

The First Annual Twig Family Reunion was held later that summer in Hickory Springs, Wyoming. There were Twigs from Ohio, and Twigs from Nebraska, Twigs from Canada and Twiggs from England. All in all, there were more than enough Twigs to make a fine looking family tree.

"Thomas Twigg would be very proud of you," her grandfather said.

"Thanks, Grandpa," she replied. "We had a great time together, didn't we?"

Emily's grandfather put his arm on her shoulder.

"We sure did. And just think, it all began with 'one tiny Twig.'"